EAST VILLAGE WABI SABI

A Novella

EAST VILLAGE WABI SABI

A Novella

ERIKA TANAKA

MOONHAW

ISBN: 979-8-9888307-1-9

Cover art by Sabina Kencana
Book design by Manuel Quintana
Epigram from Vincent van Gogh's letter to brother Theo, from Arles, Summer 1888; as quoted in *Vincent van Gogh*, edited by Alfred H. Barr; Museum of Modern Art, New York, 1935.

Printed and bound in the USA
First printing September 2023

Published by Moonhaw Press
2368 Route 214
Lanesville, NY, 12450

moonhaw.com

For all the invisible teachers

I envy the Japanese the extreme clarity that
everything in their work has...
Their work is as simple as breathing.

Vincent Van Gogh

IN THE REARVIEW (the only mirror she dared glance in these days), Mrs. McArthur saw herself raw and weathered. She'd first sighted The Paint Me Yours while turning away from that repulsive image on her way to do the shopping. Tucked in the far corner of the strip mall across from the Turpin Hills Costco, it announced itself with a sign decorated with artsy font and paintbrushes.

That font, that place, had been tethered to her attention for months. Each time she loaded up the trunk of the Liberty with one-pound containers of spinach, a twelve-pack of lightbulbs, and a sheet cake that serves 48 people for $18.00, she fantasized about going in.

Without fail, Tuesday was shopping day. Four Tuesdays a month for approximately six months meant she'd dismissed the idea of going into the pottery place at least twenty-four times. During her only visit to the Big Apple (during the Clinton years), she had sighted one of these funky do-it-yourself-pottery stores in a trendy downtown area. She longed to create but didn't have the time or patience for it anymore. But something about the perfectly manufactured colorless forms, just waiting to be brushed with her personality, stirred something about herself she'd all but forgotten.

It was May when the lightning bugs came out to zap at twilight. Perhaps because the invitations for her son's high school graduation had gone out or because she had gotten drunk on white wine on her back porch alone last night watching the insects' little green lights constellate above her lawn. For whatever reason, today, Mrs. McArthur was feeling unusually bold. Today, she went in.

Regret commenced the moment the little bell affixed to the door jingled at her. She hesitated, almost recoiled, at the shelves crammed with albino piggy banks, curvaceous vases dressed in wedding gowns, rearing unicorn candlestick holders, and Lord and Savior-shaped cookie jars. Then, a bowl as perfectly formed as a galaxy caught her eye.

"That bowl costs twenty bucks," yawned the twenty-something employee with that art student look all the kids were subscribing to nowadays.

Her hair was the color of kumquats, and a paintbrush was tattooed inside her elbow. She wiped her hands on her khaki smock.

"Plus twelve for the kiln fee."

Mrs. McArthur drew out her checkbook, printed with pictures of Persian kittens and the name HENRY J. MCARTHUR, and scratched out a check for twenty-two bucks, plus tax. The laboriousness of the antiquated transaction irritated the employee, who pulled a piece of bubblegum from her smock pocket, ripped it open, and started smacking.

Into the bright, high-ceilinged room, she swept, cradling her new bowl like a shy bather spreads her towel against her hips. She felt alive as the old transgressive spirit of adolescence returned. Smiling, she recalled the days before she met Henry. Before they took out the mortgage on the split level, before they began breeding, before she gave up her girlish dream of being an artsy-type in the big city who fell in love with interesting men, before she joined the PTA and the doctor diagnosed her with Type II Diabetes.

She squatted alone at the farthest square table covered with butcher paper, away from the birthday parties and the assisted living seniors on excursion. She gathered up all the blue paint in the studio. Blue, like the Ohio sky spreading over the highway on the drive to and from the store. Blue, like the walls of her childhood bedroom. Blue, like her husband's baseball jersey, back when he'd only been her crush. Blue, like her first and only son's squinty eyes in labor and delivery.

For twenty-two minutes, Mrs. McArthur forgot them all and simply glazed blue.

Henry Jr. graduated from Ohio State with a 3.1 GPA and a plan to move to Manhattan to figure out his plan.

"It's a shitty GPA," he whined to his parents at brunch after the ceremony. "You may have to help out with rent 'til I can find a job that I like that also pays well."

His mother swallowed her eggs Benedict whole while beaming unnaturally at him. Junior plucked out the silver-red and grayish-black strands from his mortarboard's tassel—he'd been the kid who ripped off ants' legs for fun. Of course, he'd forgotten all about that now. But his mother hadn't, though she loved her son more than the moon.

"And, you know, like, I'm never going to get a good job," Junior continued. "Everybody in New York went to the Ivy League. *And* graduate school."

"That's not true, son!" cried Senior. He'd already consumed everything on his plate except for the salad. "You double-majored in economics *and* drama—such an unusual but sensible combination, not like your mother, silly goose, who only majored in fine art. No, my boy, you'll do just fine in the Big Apple. Once you decide what you want to do, of course."

The mother had other ideas. She hadn't been listening. She was deeply invested in what her husband teased as her "food tunnel," but when she heard the swipe at her art career, her ears re-engaged. She ignored her husband's disparaging of her younger self and switched the focus to interrogating her son.

"Are you going to stay with that pretty cheerleader of yours now that school's over? What's her name, Ashleigh? Is that right?"

"No, Mom. Ashleigh and I are through. I'm going to New York as a free man."

Senior smiled. He thought this was healthy and clapped his son on the back approvingly.

"That's my boy! And you better come back one, too. I don't want no big-city liberal daughter-in-law, you hear?"

Two weeks later, Senior loaded Junior's possessions into the Liberty. He was proud that he could send his boy into the adult world debt-free to pursue his dreams for a year or two, even dreams as self-centered as acting. Young men had to sow their oats (professionally and personally). It was the only way American men were made.

Mrs. McArthur's boys piled into the leathery vehicle, dreading the long miles of close confinement, exacerbated by the father's feeble attempts at male bonding and the son's fascistic management of the Bluetooth radio. The engine sprang to life, causing Mrs. McArthur to sprint out of the kitchen via the three-car garage, her varicose veins shining like long rivers snaking down old-style parchment maps. To the men's horror, she brandished a hideous blue ceramic bowl. It was ugly. Obscure. Her husband did not roll down the window. With doughy fists, she pounded on the thin glass pane separating her from her son.

"Wait, Junior! Take this! I made it for you!"

"What the…"

"It's a *bowl*, dear. I glazed it for you at the new do-it-yourself ceramics place. See? I've inscribed your name and graduation date at the bottom. I thought you could use it to eat noodles, like we had when we went to Chinatown during our trip to the big city, remember? *Rayman,* I think the Orientals call it."

"Thanks, Mom."

The bowl was shoved through the window. Then, Mrs. McArthur noosed her son by the neck and kissed him. The husband was glad she wasn't kissing *him*.

"You be a good boy out there, Junior. Some things can't be learned from books or teachers, and I sure as heck hope you learn them—the Good Lord knows I didn't."

Junior rolled his eyes at Senior and tossed the bowl haphazardly into the backseat. It landed on a pile of hoodies and nested. It did not break. Disappointment. Then anger.

The Liberty's engine revved for real this time, and the male bonding commenced.

The first thing Junior did that summer was stop eating solid food. Everyone in the East Village was pale and thin or dark and thin but slim with matchstick legs in shorts that stopped above the knee. Junior's muscles and non-ironic baseball caps had to go. He achieved this with a week-long cleanse of cold press juices and three trips to the thrift store.

Soon, he wore tie-dye, slogans, and cuffed pipe-cleaner jeans. He claimed the mantle of veganism and regularly frequented the donation-only yoga place on St. Marks. There, he met many girls in crisscross sports bras and sheer-paneled leggings. Their flexibility reminded him of Ashleigh. They deliberately put their perfectly pumiced heels in his handsome face during Three-legged Dog.

At Mud, his favorite coffee shop, the anorexic barista studying East Asian philosophy at NYU took to calling him *McArt*, then just plain *Art*. As for his mother's blue bowl, he kept it by the bed and stashed condoms and lighters in it.

By the end of his third week as a New Yorker, Art buzzed his crew cut, tattooed a small triangle on his index finger, and purchased head shop incense to burn in his room after the yoga girls finished moon-saluting on his mattress. Kyle, his roommate, pretended not to care who came and who went. Every morning, he'd stumble into

11

the tiny corridor wearing his SpongeBob boxers, spark a roach, and rumble around in the fridge for kombucha. Kyle was a coding virtuoso from Idaho who'd dropped out of Conn U. to start a start-up that had already been started—something like Shazam for nature. *See a tree and want to know what kind of tree it is? Shazam-for-nature-it!*

The venture had flat-lined from the start. However, Kyle did have the Silicon Valley genius-intern look down: flabby arms, freckles, black shirt, lazy attitude, and never-matching socks. His sexuality was a mystery, like his proclivity for the word "extra" and ability to pay the rent every month. But both boys smoked weed, so they bonded at once by hauling found furniture off the streets and getting baked on the roof after wedging the emergency door open with a beer can. All night, they'd gaze uptown and then downtown, wondering existentially about which building was the Chrysler and which was the Empire State.

At the end of June, Art gave up acting. He *hated* his improv class. Clucking like a chicken or waiting for a nuke to go off with a fist up his ass made him feel like a five-star fool. Acting, he decided, was passé. But music corresponded to his underlying principles of existence, the monotheistic notion of his mother's idea of God. Through music, a man could touch the creative eternal. He bought a second-hand guitar in Hell's Kitchen and picked a few chords daily on the stoop beside Mud. All the neighborhood girls noticed how his beanie covered part of his infinite blue eyes. His melancholy magnetized.

The boys' air conditioner broke when August arrived with its stickiest heat. Kyle sped off to Fire Island with some dude friends that Art "didn't know." He was alone.

It was too hot to sleep. He stopped going to yoga even though it meant giving up on sleeping with the hot, ambiguously Asian girl with the sickest Full Wheel he'd ever seen. When he'd exhausted the dating apps, and it was still too hot to sleep, he stayed up scrolling through the news on his phone. He read a story about a pro-meat protestor in London who ate a live squirrel in public and decided veganism was over. After that, his new evening ritual consisted of devouring foot-longs at Papaya Dog on St. Marks until a girl from the neighborhood walked by, wanting him to take her home.

The girls he fucked that summer only had two things in common: they all wanted him to be their boyfriend, and they all had air conditioning.

Leaves turned.

Kyle found a nine-to-five tech job artfully obscuring "exotic" concepts behind a standing desk in Dumbo. Mr. and Mrs. McArthur called every Sunday after church to tell their son, "We're praying that Jesus will find you a good job and a good girl soon."

Jesus hadn't found him shit. Junior's music sucked. He hadn't written a single song. He briefly considered poetry. But after a night of Poetry Slam with some lesbians who didn't put out in the Lower East Side, he decided that writing, unlike him, was queer. Still, he refused to assimilate to what the world expected of him. He couldn't articulate it, but the necktie's specter, his future as his father's ghost, haunted him like a noose. Deep in his DNA, he harbored a kind of past life memory of corporate lynching, so he *had* to keep pursuing other

15

ways of living or die. He wasn't *trying* to be melodramatic, but explaining what he was trying to do to his parents would simply diminish it. "Imposter!" they would cry when he told them who he wanted to be now. Genuineness was the only goal he harbored now.

He wanted to be different from the "fauxgi's" who wore white kaftans and beads to chase size-zero enlightenment, the shaved-headed wannabe models who painted on cardboard boxes and sold weed but dated investment bankers, and the reggae producers hibernating in cafes wearing headphones. The vitreous layer of bullshit encompassing their human minds and all of its "unnatural" thoughts were the same; they'd all studied something that gave them the capacity to become quite clinical. Yet, if questioned, they would munch on kale, deny it, and quote Rumi.

Stop acting so small. You are the universe in ecstatic motion. That'll be $17.50 for the beet-parsley juice.

Already, New York was beginning to lose him. Or was he losing New York? Maybe the critics were always right.

To fund his juice habit, Art took a job at a formerly trendy spot on East 9th— Curvilinear. It was a stupid sake place with an S-shaped bar that tried hard with lights and decor to be cool but just wasn't. Art feared he was losing glimpses of his value; creativity was only a right so long as newness and youth persisted. His time to become *somebody*, like his half of the rent furnished by his mother, was running out.

The wet cold came in October. It was the kind of rain that almost becomes snow but tricks you because it's just freezing rain. Nobody was on the streets. Nobody drank sake anymore. Infused vodka was again having a moment now. Curvilinear's only regular was a middle-aged white guy whom Art had secretly dubbed "Ol' Yeller Fever" because he got drunk on Japanese beer, consumed exclusively manga, and swore he'd journey to Kyoto one day and bring back his sixteen-year-old Samurai-warrior-princess bride.

Ol' Yeller Fever never tipped, so Art consoled himself with the belief that fiscal brokenness was one of success' teleological benchmarks. *I have to have something to say in the Forbes interview one day.* He wiped down the bar, incredulous that he had three more hours until his shift ended. *I wonder what Ashleigh's doing right now. Who she's fucking.*

The bar's front door soundlessly cracked open. A small form cloaked in what appeared to be an irregular-shaped, rough-surfaced black nylon bag shook like a dog, then shuffled across the floor. Modest and humble, it unsheathed before a stool to reveal a rail-thin, middle-aged Japanese woman with a still-pretty face and shoulder-length hair streaked sidewalk gray. Her exact age was indeterminate (somewhere between forty-five and sixty), and her beauty was the beauty of things unconventional. In an urban way, she emanated the rustic and was dressed in idiosyncratic solutions: old Levi's and a black linen smock covered in white dust. A packet of American Spirits poked out from one of the marsupial pockets. On a pragmatic level, the woman was either a good baker or a bad coke dealer. On the philosophical-spiritual, she was some sort of doctrine only transmitted from mind to mind.

19

Undisturbed by Ol' Yeller Fever's creepy gaze, which fell on her hard, the woman crept toward the bar and shimmied onto the stool. Her feet hovered and did not touch the ground. They raked the air like a little kid's. She wore the most beat-up sneakers Art had ever seen. He wondered if she'd stained them with teabags to get them distressed like that. He marveled at this aura-enshrouded soul: She was no imposter.

The mystery woman leaned into the light, tapping the bar to let Art know she was ready to imbibe. Her skin looked a little blue. She coughed, then covered her mouth with her hands. Shallow rifts split her nails, and flakes of what looked like clay clumped in her cuticles.

"Kamoizumi," she said, then coughed again.

"Kamikaze?"

Everything the Japanese customers said sounded like "kamikaze" or "gyoza" to Art. Whenever he echoed back that stock foreign language lexicon, he was usually rewarded with knowingly appreciative grins, *ahhh so*'s, and bigger tips. Not with her.

"That's racist," replied the woman, though it sounded like *lacist*. She pointed to the unfiltered sake section on the menu.

"Sorry. I didn't mean to...I mean, you know what I mean. Kamoizumi coming right up."

She drained two in as many minutes, then nursed the third. She squatted on that stool like a solitary fisherman in his hut alone on the twilight shore, slouching and speaking to no one. If she had a phone, she did not use it. She savored each sip in stony silence.

Art had never seen anything so elusive before. Despite her elegance derived from explicit avoidance, nothing was prissy or dilettantish about her. In between each round, she did not pull her coat back around her tiny body but shuttled outside and throttled an American Spirit like it was a ghost.

She paid her bill in cash—exact change and a twenty-two percent tip. Meanwhile, Ol' Yeller Fever had given up on the exotic stranger and gone to CVS to buy antihistamines and Doritos. Last call was less than an hour away. The Japanese woman crouched outside beneath the bar's awning, doing her best to shield one last cigarette from the sideways ice rain before shuffling home. Art swilled a little shochu, abandoned his post beside the stacked-up imported casks, and trotted outside.

"Hey," he said, pulling out one of his Marlboro Reds. He waved the pack at her to indicate how he *hated* cigarette bums. "Can I steal a light?"

She did not look at him but supplied the flame.

"So, do you, like, live around here?"

"Work."

"Oh yeah? Are you, like, an artist or something?

"Some-sing."

"Where are you from?"

"Here."

"No, where are you *from*."

Silence for at least ninety seconds, then, "Japan."

"Oh, cool! I'd like to go there someday and see the temples. I'm from Ohio."

For the first time, the woman looked at him. She was paying maximum attention to him. He didn't like it. It made him feel small and a little bit scared. Naked, but not in a "my-dick-is-big-and-I'm-about-to-please-you-with-it" kind of way.

"In my language, ohayou means 'good morning.' Ohayou gozaimasu."

He brightened. When she spoke Japanese, she sounded like a bird singing. Since he'd moved to New York, he'd not heard much of that, birds singing. Maybe he'd tell his mother as much next Sunday. Better not. She'd probably saw down the nearest nest, taxidermy a baby robin, and FedEx it to him.

"Ohio gyoza. I'll remember that. So, what kind of art do you do?"

"Ser-am-ick."

She pulled a business card from her smock pocket, but not the one where she kept the cigarettes. Both meticulous and messy at the same time. Art examined the card.

"Oh, I know the place. It's just at the end of the block, right before the corner. You said your name was Yoko. Did I hear that right? Wah-bee-Sah-bee Ceramics. What does it mean?"

She shook her head, then hesitated as if she was about to offer a few apologetic words about how difficult it was to explain. But instead, she just half-smiled and said, "Come by and see."

In the mid-70s, the woman whom Art called "Yoko" had defied her parents and extricated herself from the Japanese Burden to move to America and become a jazz singer. The youngest daughter of post-war parents who claimed to be the descendants of samurai, her mother had been devastated to learn of her only daughter's Occidentalism. The father, however, had only feigned furiousness. Really, he'd always disliked his youngest child because his own father, the girl's ojisan and a religious man, had favored her. The father was, therefore, somewhat relieved to be rid of such an unfilial daughter.

As a young expat newly arrived in the nexus of the world, she'd found an unrecorded job placing noodles of ambiguous Asian origin before white patrons struggling to wield chopsticks in the West Village. All day, she served them illegally, then crawled home on aching feet to a leaseless futon crammed onto the living room floor of a medium-sized three-bedroom apartment on Avenue D. The Apato, as the place was known, welcomed paperless iconoclasts newly arrived from Japan with the same compassionate austerity with which the Eihei-ji Temple in the Fukui Prefecture received Western tourists. Everybody received a list of rules upon arrival. Visitors dressed modestly and kept silent in the common areas. Sleeping in and photography of roommates and their work were prohibited. Phone calls to parents were given priority over phone calls to lovers. No one was allowed to reside there for more than ninety days.

By the time the Department of Housing got wind of the city's least obtrusive artistic squatter's community, raided the place, and Bill de Blasio deported a Japanese jazz quartet, more than one thousand Japanese photographers, actors, and painters had curled up, and wept privately on The Apato's tidy futons.

Yoko's ninety days passed quickly. New York City jazz clubs did not book singers who sang beautifully in English but did not properly speak it. Silly accents between sets tainted a singer's aura—unless she was Australian, Russian, or Latina. Asian girls were best seen, not heard. Somewhere around day seventy-two, while working a double shift at the restaurant, Yoko noticed that the Americans were more impressed by the ceramic bowls than the noodles coiled inside them. The gaijin tongue had no appreciation for subtlety or umami, but they fawned over the novelty of crooked, cracked earthenware. They called it *rustic, quaint,* and *pleasingly naïve* and constantly asked her where they could buy some.

When Yoko had been a little girl growing up in the Ibaraki Prefecture, her ojisan, a minerally man with a Meiji Era mustache, had taught her how to throw clay and turn the kick wheel counterclockwise, allowing the rocking motion of her body to determine the asymmetry of the bowl. She had spent many holidays rolling clay with her grandfather, shaping bowls only for him to smash them without a quiver of his mustache. She never made one thing he did not break because it was not imperfectly perfect enough. Still, she had understood his discipline as attention, which is love. Once, after a long day in his studio, she was kneeling in his tatami lap while he smoked his pipe. She would never forget this haloed image of him like a Russian Orthodox icon, wearing his black robes smeared with white clay dust like sacred ash.

"Make potsu, not artu," Ojisan had advised her.

Because of her industrious politeness and madam-like presiding over the younger girls, when her 90 days were up, Yoko was never evicted from The Apato. Instead, she became its abbess and stored all her tips inside a kazaridaru, which she'd been given by a friend who curated an exhibition at The Japan Center on Second Avenue about the role of sake barrels at Shinto shrines. Like most events at the Japan Center, it was attended only by lonely expats and overzealous white men hoping to find complacent, much younger wives with little to no knowledge of English.

By the time Yoko finally saved up enough tips to lease a retail space on East 9th Street, the year was 1982. She swept out the dead cockroaches, laid non-lethal traps for the mice, drilled holes in the wall to hold up wooden shelves, brought in a kick wheel and a gas kiln, threw clay, glazed bowls, and sold them for cash, wrapped in scraps of *The Village Voice*. She quickly found her ojisan's rhythm in the pottery and learned how to make pieces he would not have smashed: solid and long-lasting, intended for everyday use.

She sank into the solitude of the process, from ball of clay to kiln. Glaze firing was her favorite. Oppressive temperatures over 2,200 degrees enthralled her. This hell-world of her own stoking was a microcosm of her Manhattan. Here, she reigned like Yama: damning, incinerating, reincarnating. She loved to watch the lumps slide onto the innermost coals as half-forms, like secrets. Instead of annihilation, their deformities reemerged impervious to the elements, ready to support eating and drinking.

For thirty years, she worked alone. Her parents got old and sick. She did not return to Ibaraki Prefecture to tend to them. She was unfilial and had no papers; if she left America, there was no guarantee she could re-enter. Her brothers kicked and screamed and erased her name from the family registry. She wore Levi's and tried not to care. Otosan then Okasan died of strokes, one right after the other. Because she did not attend the funerals, she commissioned a Japanese carpenter acquaintance who lived in Rhinebeck to make her a butsudan at a discounted rate, explaining that she needed the small wooden cabinet to protect her gohonzon now that her parents had returned to the ancestors. Even though her brothers did not ship over her share of their parents' bones, she set up the shrine in a corner at the back of the shop, near the kiln, and spoke to it regularly, saying things like, "I'll be back soon," whenever she went out, or "I am home," when she returned. She made special cups to offer her ancestors ocha each morning. The handleless kind, shaped like beehives. But she never made instruments for the tea ceremony. She wouldn't dare.

Eventually, Americans discovered matcha and feted its wellness qualities. Sales of her beehive cups (which customers extolled on Yelp as "authentic tea ceremony stuff") exploded. For a while, she had enough money to hire a young employee, a second-generation Korean student with a hard mouth and gentle raven eyes. Just in time, too, for the long years of smoking and laboring at the wheel and kiln had infected Yoko's lungs with potter's rot, a form of exacerbated grinder's asthma. The Chinese doctor had ignored it, but the Western doctor was alarmed and warned, "If left untreated…"

She left the doctor without filling his prescription because she could not pay the $748 sticker price without insurance. The next day, she fired the Korean and blamed it on a beehive on the floor in pieces.

The girl swore she had not cracked a thing, but Yoko sneered, "I know you did it on purpose."

When the girl left in tears, Yoko swept up the cup she'd accidentally smashed herself while sweeping up the night before, lit a stick of incense, and muttered to the butsudan in Japanese, "It is for the best, anyway. *Time Out* says that pomegranate juice is threatening to overtake matcha as the latest craze. I need to cut back on expenses."

From then on, Yoko worked alone. She did not qualify for Obamacare. The Western doctor's bills mounted.

The rusty bell on the door, which paid close attention to ritual, rang to announce his arrival. Yoko was summoned out of the back room, where she had been throwing a salad bowl, and wiped her hands on her linen apron.

"Can I help you?" *Help* sounded like *harp*.

The boy waved her business card between his index and middle fingers like one of his Marlboros.

"Remember me? Art from Curvilinear."

"Yes, Artu-san, I remember. What can I do for you?"

He circumambulated slowly around the shop, pretending to inspect the bowls and cups. The atmosphere derived its desolation from melancholy. Such sad, little monochromatic shops initially gave the neighborhood its 9th- and 10th-century Chinese poetry charm. But the sense dissipated quickly like an ink painting left out in the rain. Art ran his fingers along a long work table covered in butcher's paper. His touch lingered on an asymmetrical soup bowl the color of a robin's egg. Next to the bowl was a bill. ConEdison: $476— plus delinquency.

"Teach me," he said suddenly with that direct, John-Wayne tone that the Japanese find so disarming.

"Excuse me?"

"How to do what you do. I'll pay you."

A long pause. Yoko drifted over to the worktable and slid the unpaid bill into her marsupial pocket, which folded alongside her cigarettes.

"It's not that kind of studio. Nothing here is mass-produced. Nothing here is entertainment."

"I want to learn wabee-sabee. I Wikipedia'd that shit after we met. The word means 'simplicity and moral principles, tea ceremonies, putting flowers in vases, blah-blah, ugliness, and nature.'"

"You don't learn. I can't teach you."

Wabi Sabi was not her life's philosophy. It was only a name meant to signify strangeness permeated with sophistication. She made potsu, not artu. But the blond boy did not leave. As a good-looking white boy with a

36

college degree, refusal of another's reality, she knew, was the right of his social art. He'd been taught that nothing could not be learned or mastered. Failing that, purchasing was always an option. Nevertheless, he did appear to be genuinely excited, and that intrigued her.

The boy lifted his long legs onto the high counter and craned there like he was the son of the official the city had sent to inspect the place. Or, a young Rikyu. The stoneware trembled. He hitched up his jeans so that his pearly ankles showed while staring at her mouth corners, softened from frowning. To him, she was like a bird settled on a low wall, hand-crafted in the old way with stones and cement into a barrier that existed between feathery neighbors in name only. Too low not to easily leap over. He ran his long, silvery finger around the rim of a cracked yellow bowl. He picked it up and turned it over.

Some Chinesey characters were carved by fingernail into the base, along with the year and the place: NYC, 1996. The year after he was born. Even though it was lumpy, a dull color, and broken, it was so much prettier than his mother's bowl. He did not know why he wanted to secure it or what he'd use it for, but his need for it intensified. He leaned in and brushed the errant hair from the woman's face. She gave him the look of a Nara doe in tour bus headlights.

"You see, Yoko," he murmured, "that's exactly what I need to learn. How to be all Zen and shit. How to do what you do and know for sure, beyond a doubt, that there is more. There's something about you that I can't stop thinking about. Those shoes. That smock. It shouldn't be, but it is. You're not like other girls. American girls. Girls my age…"

She knew what he really wanted: crude, indigenous, anonymous. But she did not want to know *why*. She had no intention of giving him what he wanted any more than an emperor wished to be given a farmer's hut of rough mud walls.

Instead, she agreed to give him the lessons.

The first thing he made was a hideous cup for holding toothbrushes dipped in arsenic. Yoko snatched it from the kiln and smashed it on the floor. Art stomped his feet and shouted at her.

"What the fuck, Yoko?"

Wordlessly, she pointed to the broom. He cut himself cleaning up the pieces. His blood was on the butcher paper on the

39

worktable, sprinkled beside another unpaid bill. Time Warner—$223.

When she did it again to the next thing he made, a little cloud-colored water dish for cats, he pouted and whined, "What's the point?"

"There is a memory of the hut in the traveler's mind. Go there."

There sounded like *Dare*.

Everything he made, she broke. This created a rift in their relationship. He thought she was jealous of his talent, but her jealousy only made him wilder. Thoughts of cornering her at the long work table invaded him as he worked. *Press her belly onto the butcher's paper, lift up her smock, and perform my own "way" upon her.* Her snow-streaked night hair would fly in his face as she protested, then acquiesced in her meek native tongue: *Don't stopu, Artu-san!*

40

In this way, ostensibly, theirs was a form of religious and spiritual training. Every week, he brought a little money. He soon realized she was feeding her unpaid bills into the fire. That was why she piled them on the workbench beside the kiln. They never spoke about a fee for the lessons. He simply stuffed into an envelope what he thought was appropriate (namely, what he thought she thought he could afford) and then left the envelope of cash atop the pile of unpaid bills. The first time he did it, the kiln's glow caught on her face and illuminated the grooves in her skin so that she looked like a very old man on the brink of death. Otherwise, communication between them remained relatively minor.

When they worked, she admonished, always, although she had no formal system for making things. As their hands cajoled the clay, the city's inhabitants rushed around them like hinterland brush combers twisting bundles of grasses into shelters. In the evening, she stoked the kiln like a sunrise. The weeks passed, but he learned nothing. Embarkation on a new day brought only misshapen objects, wrinkled, bent, and a little cancerous looking. He kneaded, sculpted, threw, molded, fired, glazed, then fired again. She took every one of his carefully considered forms and broke them into ten thousand pieces.

"Think less," she commanded him from behind the wheel. "Don't make decisions. Artistic or otherwise."

Art's bowls got lumpier. He hated himself. He hated her. All she had to do was look at an ugly object to coax beauty out of it. *How?*

Snow fell.

Yoko's kiln roared all night, every night. By and by, pottery and sake began to supplant the importance of his conventional way of looking at things. Kyle wondered what was happening to his bro.

By Christmas, the bands of muscle at Art's lower back soldered. He was no longer supple. His toes eluded him while exhaling into a half-lift. His libido devolved. He observed nature and found he wanted to fuck it less. When he went home for the holidays, Mrs. McArthur worried. How thin her son was! How frail! What's this? A tattoo?

He returned to New York early in the New Year, even more removed from all things commercial and mainstream. Overlooked details seduced him, but he did not know how to put them into his pottery any more than he had figured out how to put them into his acting or guitaring. The ambiguously Asian girl with the gravity-defying Full Wheel noticed that the handsome midwesterner had disappeared from the juice shops, thrift stores, and yoga studios. She haunted the blocks like a koi in a corporate lobby pond, searching for him. When she found him existential and lonely, she wanted him even more.

She simplified her dress to suit his evolution, came to Mud every day, ordered a matcha latte and a vegan donut, and sat on a bench reading a second-hand copy of Trollope she'd purchased at the Strand, waiting for him to notice.

Months passed. He got rid of all that was unnecessary. He dressed more simply. His favorite jeans, uncuffed, soft, and stretched at the knees, were permanently speckled with clay. He abandoned slogans on t-shirts and threw out all his hats. His white sneakers wore out in their own time. They became mucked with clay and dirt. Kyle snapped at him to clean them one evening when he tracked half-dried clay smeared with dog shit into their apartment, but Art didn't care enough to interfere with natural processes.

One night, after Yoko had annihilated Art's most unpretentiously irregular salad bowl to date and made him sweep up the littered bones, he was in line at the bodega buying stale raisin bread and thinking about not-thinking, *hard*.

"I love your sneakers," a pretty redhead in the buckskin boots of the season said to him. "They're perfectly distressed. Where did you get them?"

He turned away from her. *Raisins are what I care about now.* But a flock of naked yoginis folded themselves back into his mind anyway. Their hard nipples offered themselves to his teeth like raisins, and he wanted to clamp down around them. Once, Yoko told him a story about a Zen monk who refused a temptress sent by his benefactress to test his solitude. *What was the moral of that story?* He followed the eye-arresting young woman out of the Yemeni grocer's, bundled her back to the apartment, and sprang at her on the couch. Kyle walked in, saw manicured feet in the air, and felt relieved.

They all shared a spliff after. Art's potters' hands were surprisingly deft and self-referential. The redhead gushed to him that she'd never experienced anything like it.

"You're even better than the guitarist I used to date," she breathed. "Those hands are the hands of a god."

She made him feel like Rodin, so it took him a few weeks to get rid of her. Winter was almost over. Still, Yoko was smashing his bowls. Faint evidence of progress. His emptiness was still not alive. He'd made nothing of reformation.

Spring's advent hinted at the original restoration of wilderness. Yoko's layers of black boiled wool peeled away. A glimpse of elbow was like the blinders coming off. Everything wore down. Their smocks slapped heavily against their thighs. Planets, stars, and family reputations trembled. The first week of March engulfed everything in a fine, wet mist. The Japanese don't trust nature, Art learned, because "the baby of spring is often stillborn."

In a week, hostile snow returned.

They ignored each other for most of the blizzarding night. He wasn't supposed to come in for a lesson, but Curvilinear closed early so the manager could make the last bus back to Teaneck. Despite the cold, Art couldn't not feel his hands move in clay for another moment. He pounded the backs of his fists on Wabi Sabi's door and begged entry with a bottle of unfiltered sake. Yoko opened it amid a coughing fit. She went to her favorite stool, where she sat and drank to drown the dry air in her throat. Art was left to pump with his foot and turn with his hands at the wheel alone. At first, he did not notice her contemplating her mortality and finishing the bottle like the moon finishes the night until, hours later, he extracted his bowl from her oven.

It was *almost* regular. And very, very blue. He remembered the cracked yellow bowl that had drawn him during his first visit to the shop. This reminded him of that for no reason. Why bother to ignore or pretend otherwise? Sun and sky. That is what it was. Imperfectly symmetrical.

He handed over his creation, and she turned it over, looking for flaws, and tapped it with her fingernail. Hard, inert, solid. She handled it like it was some intangible thing. He knew the smash was coming but wouldn't care this time. He *hated* that bowl. It was imperfect because it purported to be perfect. It was laziness and deserved to be destroyed. Oblivion faded from Yoko's face. With his fingernail, the boy had scratched something that had come to him onto the bowl's underside: *What is the lesson of the universe?*

In that cold, lowly environment, the woman whom the boy called Yoko faced the conditions of what she'd always considered ugly. She could still see the chin of her first white customer waggle as she placed a bowl of noodles before him. He'd grabbed her wrist, grinned, and called her a "foxy chink."

With her back to the boy, Yoko lit a stick of incense and offered it to the butsudan.

"I am making potsu," she whispered.

Autumn musk mixed with maple filled the shop. Then, she lit an American Spirit and gazed at her ward in an alerted state—the way Otosan had looked at her when she told him she was leaving Japan because Japan had nothing for women like her. Art's lushness bloomed. How had she failed to notice? The young man before her was rough and flawed as the maple tree twisting through the concrete at the end of the block where she'd grown up. His bowl was homely but not repulsive. She wondered if she should sing for him, just once. She opened her mouth, and a melody came out, not in English, as intended, but in Japanese.

Is the plant complete when it flowers? When it goes to seed?

When she was done, he rushed at her, and she snatched the waistband of his jeans like a samurai snatched his sword. Any invisible tissue that removed them from each other was peeled away. His skin was off-white as unbleached cotton. Hers was yellow and see-through.

They did not linger in each other's arms or light cigarettes immediately after. She fetched water, boiled it, prepared the tea, and served it to him. She poured the remainder into a beehive, then placed it on the porch of the butsudan. He rested his head in her naked lap so that the thicket of her bush tickled his ear. He pointed to the small cabinet.

"I've always wondered, what is that?"

"Shrine. For my dead family."

"Is that why you talk to it? Because you miss them?"

He could not decipher her straight smile.

"No. Because of respect."

Snow melted.

Strange, indecisive winds blowing north along the coast warmed the morning and dissolved it all away.

In the evening, Art hurried under the withered branches beneath the almost spring sky, willing, *Cherry blossoms, come soon.*

Because of a fear he could not name, he did not stop by the next day or the next. On the third, Art bought a dozen bodega roses to offer to Yoko to offer to her dead. He raced toward her shop, evanescent, ready to make love on the worktable again and then make a vase he had woken up with in his mind. He was going to glaze it silver-red grayish black. The color he'd seen behind his eyelids when they'd made love. A gift for her.

In the store window, she'd put out green-brown mugs, which he'd never seen before, along with a sign. *SALE: EVERYTHING 50% OFF.* The lump he hadn't even realized was lodged in his throat suddenly felt like clay ablaze in the kiln.

For the first time in his life, Art had everything he wanted, and now, the bitch was just giving it away? The young American man was in love, and not just with a woman. It was too much emotion to jam through a small verbal frame. How he felt about what he knew was a haiku. But acceptance of the inevitable did not mean he was prepared to share it.

The door was locked. Yoko was not there. He smoked three cigarettes in thirteen minutes. A fat pigeon came and scratched. A rat scurried. A young mixed-race couple walked by wearing cuffed jeans and matching Fitbits. They were kissing and laughing. *Not all existence shares the same fate*, he thought. Then, he didn't want to not-think anymore. His patience was a twilight shore.

He threw the roses to the ground and was about to leave when a young Korean girl with a pleasing moon face and a tidy, tanned California body swished out; she'd been hiding in Yoko's backroom all this time. Doing what? She peeked at the discarded flowers, then into Art's cobalt eyes, and blushed.

"Hey, miss, who are you?"

"Uh-um, I'm Ms. Nonaka's former employee. Who are *you*?"

"Her apprentice."

"Huh? I thought she didn't teach. It's not like she's some Zen master or anything."

"Then why are *you* here?"

"Because she called me late last night and asked if I could, like, come by and take care of a few things. She wanted the windows changed and that sale sign put out. Retail," she rolled her eyes. "You know how it goes."

"No, actually, I don't. Where is she?"

"She didn't tell you? She's in the hospital. Don't worry, she'll be, like, totally fine."

Rice paper ripping. The forlorn bellow of foghorns. Ambulances screaming through canyons between high-rises. And just like that, the European cathedral of the boy's first transcendent feelings came crashing down. The Korean didn't notice any inner turmoil at all. She just grinned at his blondeness bashfully.

"I'd *love* to hear more about what you two are studying. I had, like, no idea she was, um, doing that. Hey, do you wanna, like, get a cortado at Mud or something?"

Art briefly considered revenge like art history students consider Modernism, but no. The Korean girl was too trifling. He figured she studied digital media at the New School and condemned her to vapidity.

On his way home, however, for the first time in a long time, he noticed the ambiguous Asian hottie. She was dressed cleanly in a navy peacoat, white cotton dress, and beat-up sneakers. Sitting quietly on the bench outside Mud, she was sipping a pomegranate juice and reading a tattered copy of Trollope, waiting.

It was April when Yoko finally came back from wherever she'd gone. Art had quit his job at Curvilinear. His lease with Kyle was about to run out, and he wasn't sure if he would renew and, if not, where he would go next. In the meantime, he still walked down East 9th every day, hoping to glimpse Yoko back at the worktable, hair and smock dangling, feet bare and white as dried, cracked clay.

Then, one afternoon, it was as if she'd never gone away. She was just there, glazing a bowl with the same sky blue he had used the night he'd made the bowl she had not broken before they'd made love.

He treaded lightly into the store. The bell screamed, announcing his presence. Incense smoldered on the porch of the butsudan. More bills than ever were piled beside her on the worktable. Medical shit. Debt collectors' threats. The kiln was heating up. She was going to bonfire all the invoices accrued while she was in the hospital, including those the hospital had dispatched while she was still being held hostage there, racking up bills she knew she could never pay. On her left wrist, she wore a hospital bracelet printed with her name like a receipt: Hito Nonaka.

He wanted to seize her by the bowed shoulders and shout: *Material poverty and spiritual richness are not the only way to enjoy an unencumbered life*!

But she coughed, and a little blood came out, so he made fists to contain his anger in his fingertips instead.

"How long have you been back?"

"Not long."

Long sounded like *wrong*.

"Are you really sick?"

"Not really."

He wanted to go to her, fold her into his arms, and rock her back and forth until

58

her sickness stopped. But then, the web of fate forced him to see it. The mechanics and dynamics of existence in pieces all over the floor—the remnants of his sky-blue bowl.

"What the fuck, Yoko? Why did you do that? That bowl was perfectly imperfect, and you know it. That's why you *fucked* me, remember? Right here, on the worktable, crinkling up the butcher's paper with your ass."

"Lesson finished. You have learned about the pleasure of things and the pleasure we get from freedom from things." *Things* sounded like *sings*.

"What is wrong with you? Crazy bitch!"

"I get rid of all that is unnecessary."

He stood in the studio and suddenly felt it all. His rage was a creative force as roaringly hellish as the kiln. For the moment, he appreciated it as just that, pure biological hatred, and an exquisite clarity surfaced: In the studio-shop, things only came into existence when they expressed their wabi-sabi qualities; when they exited and returned to ordinary reality, their wabi-sabi faded away. He could still be anything he wanted—a wealthy businessman, poor student, struggling musician, or powerful religious leader. It was *she* who was no longer of consequence. Illness warped, discolored, and shriveled her. Nicked, chipped, dented, scarred, and peeled her. The argument was the same as the NRA's in favor of more guns to combat more guns: It was not illness that misused bodies, but people.

"Sweep, please, before you go." *Please* sounded like *prease*.

He fetched the broom and knelt amid his shards. He picked up a large fragment and cradled it like a scientist might a frontispiece that he has dug up and declared once belonged to a Neanderthal skull. Thick and heavy in his hand, the shard still possessed undiminished poise and strength of character. In this state, Art's creation was more beautiful than the complete bowl had ever been.

Why couldn't she see it? No, she would never be able to exhibit the effects of his accident. *Jealous bitch*. Perhaps she knew he had considered fucking the Korean. Yes, yes, that was it! Treachery in the South Pacific! The slut had told her all about it. Lies derived from incompleteness of understanding.

Desperately, he wanted to get close to Yoko, Hito, or whatever her name was. But she was bent over the butsudan, talking to it in Japanese. Every atom of him demanded attention. *I am important!* He seethed to relate. To reduce the psychic distance between them. To touch her on the table.

61

The low ceilings lowered. The small windows shrank. The tiny shop entrance closed. The studio fell tranquil, womb-like, like Nagasaki after The Bomb. The green ready-light on the kiln flickered on. Provenance was nowhere, anywhere, and everywhere. Every object in the place suddenly seemed to expand in importance in inverse proportion to its actual size. The big ones, like human beings and the butsudan, mattered least. She turned around in time to see him, just as he was. Confusion. Fear. Medication. A tumescent bud with silver rust.

She was too blurry to cry out, "Artu-san! What are you doing?"

But he. He was his background and personality, every facet of it—coarse, unrefined, and ready for infinity's mass production. A blue fucking bowl.

Two years later, Mr. and Mrs. McArthur finally came to New York to meet their son's partner. Mrs. McArthur, especially, had a delightful time. She visited all the museums, like the Metropolitan and MoMA, and felt reinvigorated. Although they stayed comfortably for an entire week in the couple's new home in Tribeca, they could not figure out how to pronounce their future daughter-in-law's multisyllabic Thai name. It had too many vowels. They referred to her in private as "Natalie" and to her face as "Nat."

Mrs. McArthur was very nervous around her. She had no idea how to relate to the daughter of a former Minister of Commerce who was often spotted in Thai fashion magazines and had come to the US to pursue a master's in digital communications at the

New School. She was rich, exotic, and read Trollope. Mrs. McArthur hated that she had to fret about remembering to take off her shoes in the apartment the girl's father paid god knows how much for.

Nevertheless, the McArthurs were thrilled with Nat's influence over their son. Nat's bureaucrat father had made a few poignant introductions on Wall Street, and their son now wore a shirt, tie, and shoes that shined. The crew cut came back, as did his physique. He enlisted for the company softball team and sparkled in his baseball cap and cotton gym bag emblazoned with the bank's logo. For their first anniversary, Nat presented Junior with an expensive Swiss watch, and he gave her a silver Tiffany necklace in the shape of infinity. It shone at her throat when she hugged his mother. It was evident to Mrs. McArthur that an engagement was not far off.

The sweeping Tribeca loft, Mrs. McArthur noted with aplomb when she arrived, was not far from the Paint Me Yours she had discovered on her first trip to New York all those years ago. She was even more delighted to see that on the mirrored credenza in the entranceway sat the ceramic blue bowl she had glazed and given her son as his graduation present several years ago.

Maternal love, something closer to personal pride, surged in her, and she flew to the bowl to touch it. However, upon closer inspection, she frowned. The bowl was cracked in ten thousand places, though it had been lovingly glued back together with golden lacquer filling in the cracks. Even crisscrossed with golden veins so that it shone like the sun when the hallway light touched it, the broken bowl seemed heavier, more solid, more ancient, and *alive* somehow than she remembered.

"Oh God, Henry loves that bowl," gushed Nat without the slightest trace of a foreign accent. "It was the only thing he wanted to bring from his East Village apartment, and can you believe it? The thing was already in pieces. Since he wouldn't throw it away, I told him he had to at least kintsugi it. So he did. He did a pretty good job for an average American kid who didn't grow up with this sort of thing, don't you think? I personally just throw things away and buy new ones. But I'm glad we didn't with this bowl. Don't you think it's much more beautiful now?"

"Yes," murmured the mother, "I hadn't realized I'd made something so…real. There's so much weight to it."

Nat nodded. "Yeah, I totally know what you mean. It's a special thing you made for your son there, Mrs. McArthur. He burns incense in it sometimes and talks to it. Like, he'll tell it, 'I'm going to the bodega,' or 'I'm back. It was a good day at the office.'"

"Goodness, how strange!"

"Not really, Mrs. McArthur. I think it just means he misses you."

The Thai princess winked, and Mrs. McArthur felt a strange surge of maternal love.

"Please, Nat dear, call me Evelyn."

The day before the McArthurs flew home was a Sunday. Thoughtful girl that she was, Nat arranged for brunch after church with Henry's former roommate, Kyle, and his new girlfriend—a half-black, half-Puerto Rican sound engineer with a 200-hour yoga teacher certificate and Silicon Valley ambitions. They were to dine at the hottest new eatery on East 9th, famous for its French Toast glazed with pomegranate-blueberry maple syrup.

The brunch party rendezvoused in the old neighborhood, and Junior hardly glanced at the boarded-up shop with the FOR RENT sign at the end of the block. They were led to their table, bypassing the considerable wait, and the two young women glowed with progress. Nat wore a silk ensemble printed with perfect florals, and Kyle's new girlfriend, a native Brooklynite, wore a black bandier top and ripped jeans. Soon, Nat hoped, they'd be best friends. The men gripped each other's forearms and laughed deeply. All three of them wore button-ups and jeans.

The pretty Latina waitress studying Russian Literature came, and the women ordered eggs. The men beamed at the young scholar and promptly took her recommendation for the French Toast with the famous blueberry glaze.

"Dude, didn't this place used to be that sake bar where you worked, Curvilinear? Remember? During that winter when you got a little weird and started making bowls and shit?"

Junior glared across the table at Kyle. "Don't curse in front of my mother, dude."

A pomegranate seed wedged itself between his teeth.

"Henry!" squealed his mother. "You never told me you went through a pottery phase! I guess I did inspire you, after all…"

Senior rolled his eyes and grinned at Nat. He slapped his palm down over the back of her hand and left it too long. She forced a grin.

"You know these 'artistic' types, dear," Senior began, "they cycle through all sorts of mistakes. That's youth for you. In my day, it wasn't really like that. Although, I guess the hippies found their way, eventually. Some of them are even trying to run the country now. The audacity of the Left! It all starts with a pot of paints and some canvas. Next thing you know, it's socialism for everyone. Thank goodness my boy here's finally straightened out like his dear old mother. I always knew he would come to his senses."

"Yeah, I guess, Dad. I don't know what else to tell you guys. It was a weird time in my life. I didn't really know who I was or what I wanted to be, so sue me. I took, like, one lesson on making bowls from this old Japanese lady. It wasn't weird or anything. Like, she taught classes, so it wasn't just me. This Korean chick who went to the New School in the class with me. She dropped out, though. Wonder what happened to her…

"Anyway. Now, I work at a bank, and who knows? Maybe one day, Nat and me, we'll move to Bangkok to be closer to her family, and I'll run a huge business of my own, and then…Woah, woah. I'm getting ahead of myself. There are more relevant things to talk about. Like the Superbowl. Or the primaries."

Kyle, meanwhile, had gone white as a silkworm. Something had come back to him while Art was talking. Something he'd almost forgotten. Less forgotten than lost in the ecstasy of whatever substances had enthralled them in their pulse that night. A Korean girl, whom Kyle had never seen before, *had* appeared at their door in the dead of night, assaulting their bell over and over again. She was full of threats and demanded to speak to Art. They could see from the monitor that she was wasted and waving half a slice of Ray's Pizza in one hand. Repeatedly, she screamed into the intercom that if Art didn't come down and confess, she'd go to the cops.

"I know what you did! I know what you did!"

Art and Kyle, meanwhile, peered down at her through the fire escape, lit another joint, smoked it, and then flicked it down at her skull, laughing. At the time, Art coyly offered up a convincing psycho's bio: "Sophomore with no scholarship at the New School, dad's a heart doctor out in Cali, met at some party in BK. I was wasted. I don't even remember her name, but it's my fault because I fucked her, and now she's obsessed."

Crazy bitch metastasis was an affliction suffered only by "hot" guys, of which Kyle was not one, so his energies related to the situation were limited. At the time, he'd accepted his roommate's synopsis of the stranger's life and character with more envy than questions.

"Yeah, dude," he must've concurred, "what a dumb slut."

But now, Kyle was done experimenting. He had a great job in tech, a competent therapist, and a hot mixed-race girlfriend. All these years later, he could still hear the hysteria crackling through the Korean girl's voice. The insanity of her speech when it first came through the intercom had stretched through the darkness and got to him. All these years later, it was still stretching until it got to him again. When it did, a cold shiver skied down his spine, and the ruddy hairs on his arm shot up.

"Holy fucking shit, you colossal bastard. You don't deserve any of it, Art. Not one fucking iota. I was there. You and the pottery thing, it was more than that..."

"Ky, you know I love you, bro, but you don't know what the fuck you're talking about."

Mrs. McArthur stepped in with forced pleasantness perfected in the Midwest. Divergence was her specialty.

"Well, boys," she chirped, "I, for one, would like to see this pottery place. Junior, perhaps this nice Chinese lady kept some of your pieces? I know I would if I were her."

"Ugh, Mom. No. Besides, it's long gone."

"Oh, why's that?"

"We walked right by it on the way in. It's that sad, empty for-lease place a few doors down with ugly green mugs in the window."

"Oh, rats. That is such a shame."

"All those places go out of business, sooner or later, Mrs. McArthur," piped up Kyle's girlfriend. "It's the ecosystem of our local economy."

It was the first time Kyle's girlfriend had spoken during the meal. Disparaging talk of the so-called "Radical Left" made her uncomfortable. Still, she had to exist at some point during this brunch and now seemed like the opportune moment.

"You see, it's all part of the typical lifecycle of New York City neighborhoods. Tragedy, first, and then farce. Artists and immigrants come and make a previously untouchable area cool, then it gets gentrified, and the ones who made it what it is get chased out. Landlords turn greedy and push rents sky-high so that no one takes the space for years, and they can get a tax write-off until a CVS or Chase Bank comes along. For instance, in Red Hook, where I grew up…"

"It's capitalism, plain and simple," interrupted Mr. McArthur. "And an empty retail space because one of capitalism's losers can't keep up with the changing costs of changing times is no tragedy, young lady. It's America." Mr. McArthur turned and whispered to his son, though everyone at the table could hear him, "I guess in Brooklyn, snowflakes come in brown."

Nat didn't like the tension among her future in-laws and wedding party. She preferred to manage her people like an architect who treats the design of an entire building like a blown-up piece of furniture.

"Hey, do you know what *I* heard? I remember reading in *The Village Voice* a few years ago that the old Japanese potter lady actually went crazy. She was here illegally, obviously. Underwater with debt, months behind in the rent, old, and broke. She had no one. One day, she just gave up! Stuck her head in the kiln. Those Japanese are always killing themselves. We Thai aren't like that. We don't self-immolate. Well, not often, and not without good reason. Anyway, they found nothing left of the head. Only the torso, melting on its knees. It's a miracle the whole place didn't go up in flames and kill everyone who lives upstairs. *That's* why the space is still empty. Not because of exorbitant rents, but because no sane entrepreneur will touch the bad business juju."

"Well, shit. Is that what happened, then?" exclaimed Kyle, throwing up his hands.

His girlfriend caught them and kissed them. He softened. But his eyes remained fixed on his former roommate. They were cold.

"What was that place called again, Art? Wubbysubby or something?"

Junior went to wipe his hands on his smock. But there was no smock. Just well-pressed cuffed jeans. He felt pissed off and a little violent, like wind, rain, fire, and so on. He pushed the blueberries around his plate. The bread soaked in the homemade blue glaze was dissolving. He hadn't noticed the plate beneath it before. It had been a while since he'd noticed such things: a leaf decomposing on the sidewalk, a volunteer digging up weeds in a community garden, or a sweater on a homeless person standing at the top of the subway stairs pierced with holes. The details were murky but beautiful.

He gently brushed the plate's rough ceramic edges with his fingers. It was glazed silver-red grayish black.

"Yea, man, that was it. Wabi Sabi."

Acknowledgments

Special thanks to Sabina Kencana for her beautiful work on the cover; Manuel Quintana for his expert design; Erin Wallace for copyediting an earlier draft; Jeff and many other East Village alumni for their "back in the day" stories; Bob for the chairlift chats; and Poodle, Robert, Joel, Lindsay, Bert, and Bill Birns for always reading and believing.

Erika Tanaka is a native New Yorker who writes short fiction and essays. She is also the author of the short story collection *Yellow City*.